Usborne Activities

100 Things to do on a Journey

Belongs to: Oscar

Sam Smith

Illustrated by Non Figg
and Molly Sage

Designed by Sharon Cooper

Edited by Sam Taplin

Signpost scramble

Can you unscramble the letters on each of the signs below to find the names of nine famous cities?

1. NOLNOD
2. DIMRAD
3. WEN ROKY
4. ORI ED ORINJEA
5. NEBRIL
6. SPAIR
7. COWOMS
8. MORE
9. DYSYEN

2

Vehicle timeline

Label these vehicles with numbers 1 to 6 to put them in the order they were first invented, using 1 for the earliest.

Sailing ship

Car

Hovercraft

Plane

Bicycle

Submarine

Hot-air balloons

Draw designs on the blank balloons.

Vehicle search

How many vehicles can you find in the jumble below?

Slithery snake

 + A game for two or more people

1. To start, one person picks an action word, but doesn't tell the others what it is. For example, you could choose the word 'skydive'.

2. The other players must try to guess what the word is by taking turns to ask the first player questions about it.

3. Until they know what the word is, they should replace it with the phrase 'slithery snake'.

4. Players can guess what the word is at any time if they think they've figured it out. Whoever gets it right gets to go next.

Safari search

Find the names of all the safari animals at the bottom in the grid below. They may be written in any direction.

L	E	O	P	B	I	G	C	A	R	D	N
C	Z	A	L	L	I	R	O	G	E	E	A
D	C	D	R	B	P	I	P	R	Y	N	O
O	E	Z	H	A	T	E	E	H	C	L	C
H	F	C	E	I	R	Z	F	I	A	R	T
Y	F	Z	U	B	P	H	Y	P	O	D	N
E	A	A	N	U	R	P	M	C	N	A	A
N	R	O	B	F	O	A	O	T	I	S	H
A	I	R	Y	F	T	D	N	C	H	O	P
L	G	N	A	A	I	A	M	A	R	E	E
N	S	E	E	L	L	Z	E	T	D	S	L
A	Z	L	E	O	P	A	R	D	Y	A	E

GORILLA
LION
ZEBRA
ELEPHANT

LEOPARD
RHINO
CHEETAH
HIPPO

BUFFALO
HYENA
CROCODILE
GIRAFFE

7

Helicopter match-up

Circle the two helicopters that are exactly the same.

Cable cars

Draw lots of people and ski equipment in these cable cars.

On safari

Can you plan a safari route to see monkeys, giraffes, elephants, crocodiles, rhinos, zebras, flamingos, leopards, lions and hippos – in that order? Visit every hideout to get a good view and don't take the same track twice.

Hideouts look like this.
Start and finish here

Spotting noises

 + A game for two or more people

1. Each person chooses something to spot and makes a silly noise to go with it. The noise shouldn't have anything to do with the thing that you have chosen, so don't choose anything as obvious as saying 'baa' when you see a sheep.

2. Each time someone spots their chosen thing, they make the noise that goes with it.

3. Everyone has to guess what each other is spotting, and the game ends when they have all been guessed.

TIP: If you're playing this in a car, don't make your noises too loud or sudden, in case you distract the driver. Try not to disturb other passengers on a train, ferry or plane either.

Voyage sudoku

The grid below is made up of six blocks, each made up of six squares. Fill in the blank squares so that every row, column and block contains all six letters of the word VOYAGE.

G			V		A
		Y			G
	O			V	
	G			A	
E			A		
V		G			Y

Tunnel traffic

Add up the boxes the vehicles in each line are carrying. The lower the total, the quicker the traffic. Which line will be fastest through the tunnel, and which will be slowest?

1.

2.

3.

4.

5.

Transport trickery

1. A bus driver was heading down a street in London. He went past a stop sign without stopping. Then he turned left where there was a sign for 'NO LEFT TURN'. Finally, he went the wrong way down a one-way street. But after all this, no traffic laws had been broken. Why not?

Answer: ....

2. How could a cowboy ride into town on Friday, stay two days, and then ride out again on Friday?

Answer: ....

3. A ferry sets out from Dublin for Liverpool. At the same time, a speedboat sets out from Liverpool for Dublin. If the ferry goes at 20 knots and the speedboat goes at 40 knots, which boat is closer to Dublin when they pass?

Answer: ....

Hidden picture

Fill in the shapes that have blue dots. What can you see?

Spot the difference

Can you spot ten differences between these two views from a train?

In my suitcase...

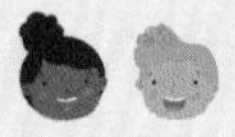

+ A game for two or more people

1. Someone begins the game by saying "In my suitcase, I have..." followed by an object. For example, you could start with "In my suitcase, I have a soggy sandwich."

2. Someone else repeats what the first person has said, then adds another object. It makes the game funnier if the objects are not related to each other in any way, such as: "In my suitcase, I have a soggy sandwich and a rusty trumpet."

3. Everyone takes turns adding items to the suitcase, each time repeating the growing list of items that are already in there. The items must be repeated in the correct order.

4. When someone forgets an item, or gets the order wrong, then that person is out of the game. The last player left in is the winner.

River route

Find the right trail to guide the canoe to the shore, avoiding the rocks.

Crossword 1

Use the clues below to fill in the correct words in the grid.

Across

3. Document to travel abroad (8)
7. Shallow ridges in the sea, often made of coral (5)
8. Something to read (4)
10. You pack things in one of these (3)
12. Travel by plane (3)
13. A place to stay (5)
14. Automobile (3)

Down

1. Hand gesture; a ripple (4)
2. Front of a boat; bend forwards at the waist (3)
4. International distress call (3)
5. What you buy to travel (6)
6. All the vehicles on the road (7)
9. Frequently (5)
10. Next to (2)
11. Opposite of bad (4)

Timely inventions

Label these important inventions in transportation and navigation with numbers 1 to 6 to put them in the order they were first used, using 1 for the earliest.

Radar

Compass

Satnav

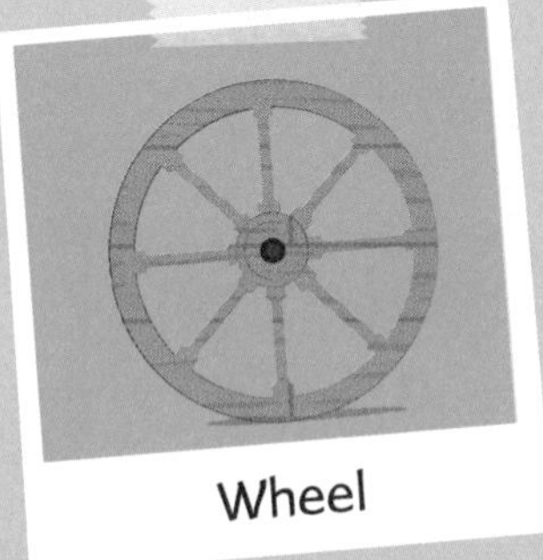

Wheel

Globe

Diesel engine

Bridge crossing

Emma, Jon, Isla and Marc need to cross a rickety old bridge to get home. The Sun is setting, and no one wants to cross the bridge without the lantern – but it's only safe for two people to cross at a time.

Each person walks at a different speed:
Emma can cross the bridge in one minute.
Jon can cross the bridge in two minutes.
Isla can cross the bridge in five minutes.
Marc can cross the bridge in ten minutes.

They only have 17 minutes to get to the other side, or they'll be late getting home. How can they do this?

Use this space for any calculations you may want to do to help you solve the puzzle.

Winding road

Draw more cars driving along this winding road.

Camping equipment

Find each item of camping equipment at the bottom hidden in the grid. Their names may be written in any direction.

P	D	C	T	U	Y	S	R	E	F	M	G
C	B	I	N	O	C	U	L	A	R	S	T
A	E	O	T	K	C	O	N	O	S	N	F
N	G	A	B	G	N	I	P	E	E	L	S
T	I	P	C	D	A	D	T	T	S	I	S
E	R	Y	A	T	E	A	L	F	S	E	A
E	A	T	O	M	C	R	A	G	A	L	P
N	M	P	E	A	O	I	M	R	L	S	M
K	C	A	P	K	C	A	B	C	G	O	O
Y	H	N	A	C	C	C	L	N	N	E	C
W	S	E	D	I	O	A	N	O	U	S	U
E	L	T	S	I	H	W	J	A	S	A	N

BINOCULARS
COMPASS
CANTEEN
JACKET
TENT
BACKPACK

SUNGLASSES
SLEEPING BAG
WHISTLE
RADIO
MAP

Quick draw

Draw a line as fast as you can from the speedboat to the pier without touching the sides.

Dock deductions

Three boats are moored at the jetty. Following the clues below, can you find out the owner of each boat, its age, and the day it arrived? Fill in your answers on the chart.

Arrived	Boat	Age	Owner
Thursday			
Friday			
Saturday			

1. *Freedom* is a year older than *Skimmer*, and isn't owned by Pete.

2. The owner of the boat that is one year old isn't Jack, who arrived on Thursday.

3. The boat that arrived on Friday is two years younger than *Mermaid*, which is owned by Sam.

4. *Skimmer* is one year old.

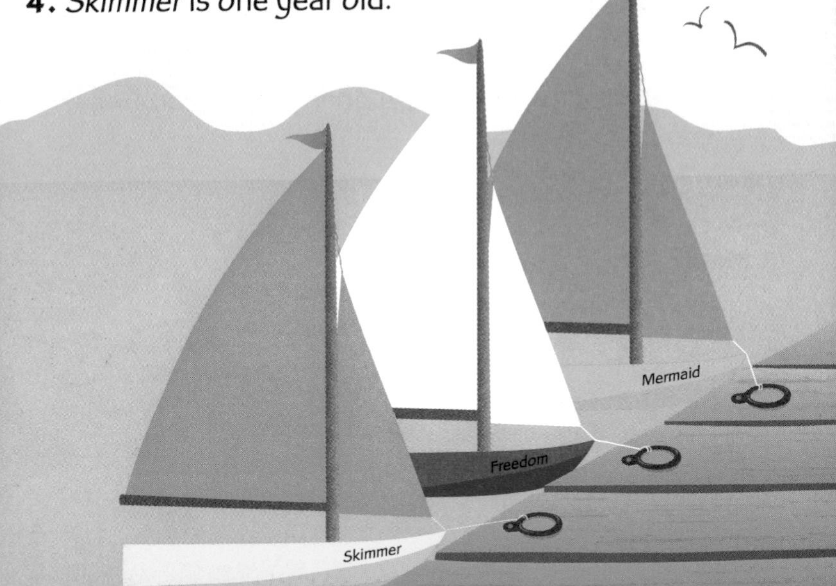

Don't say 'YES!'

A game for two people

1. One person asks the other a question to which 'yes' is the obvious answer. For example, they might ask 'Are your eyes blue?'

2. The second person answers the question without saying 'yes' in any part of their answer. In this example, they might say 'Well, they're very light blue – almost silvery, really.'

3. The game continues with the first person asking questions and the second person answering them. If the second person makes a mistake and says 'yes' then it becomes their turn to ask the questions.

TIP: Try asking someone a question that needs to have a long answer, followed by one where 'yes' is the easiest answer. If you do this, you may find it easier to catch them out.

Plane trails

Circle the plane that has come from the empty hangar.

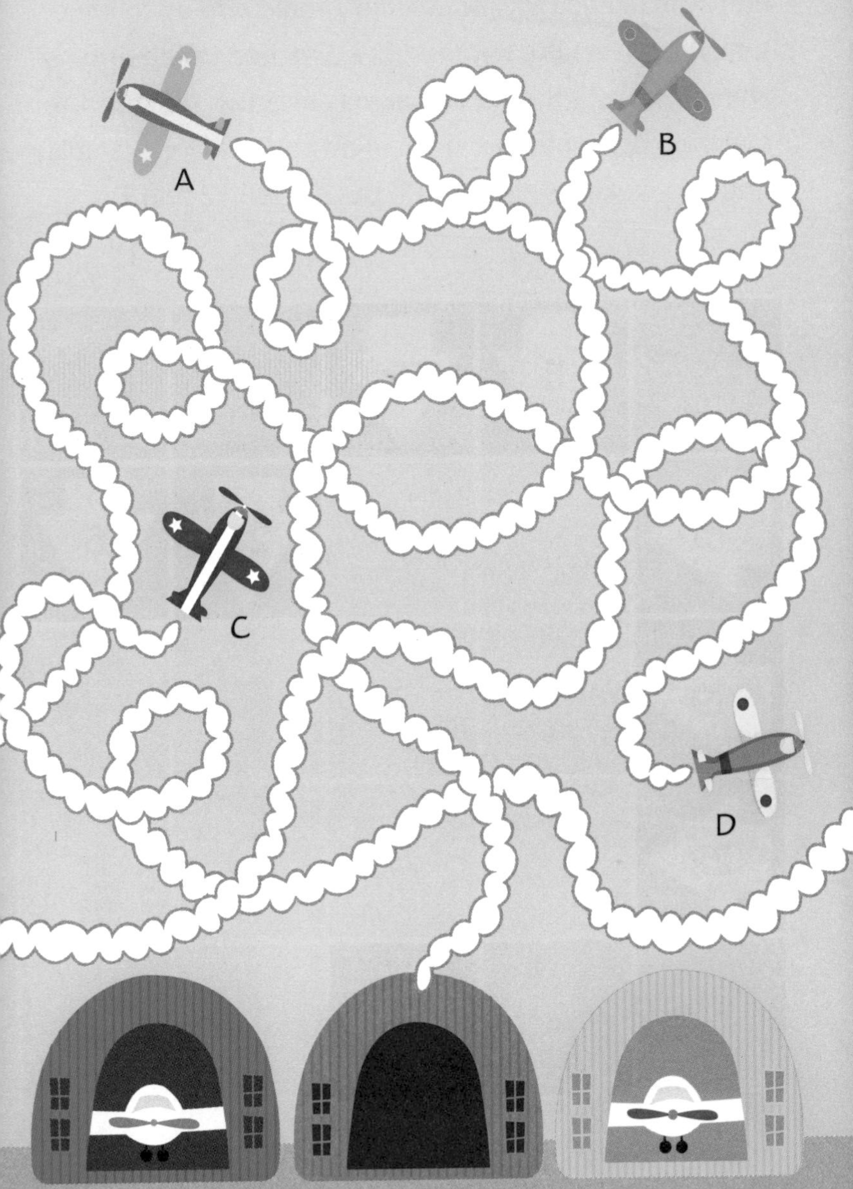

Cross sum

Fill in the blank squares with numbers from 1 to 9. The numbers in each row or column should add up to the total shown on the arrows. (The direction of the arrows shows you whether to add across or down the grid.) You can only use a number once in an answer. For example, you can make 4 with 3 and 1, but not with 2 and 2.

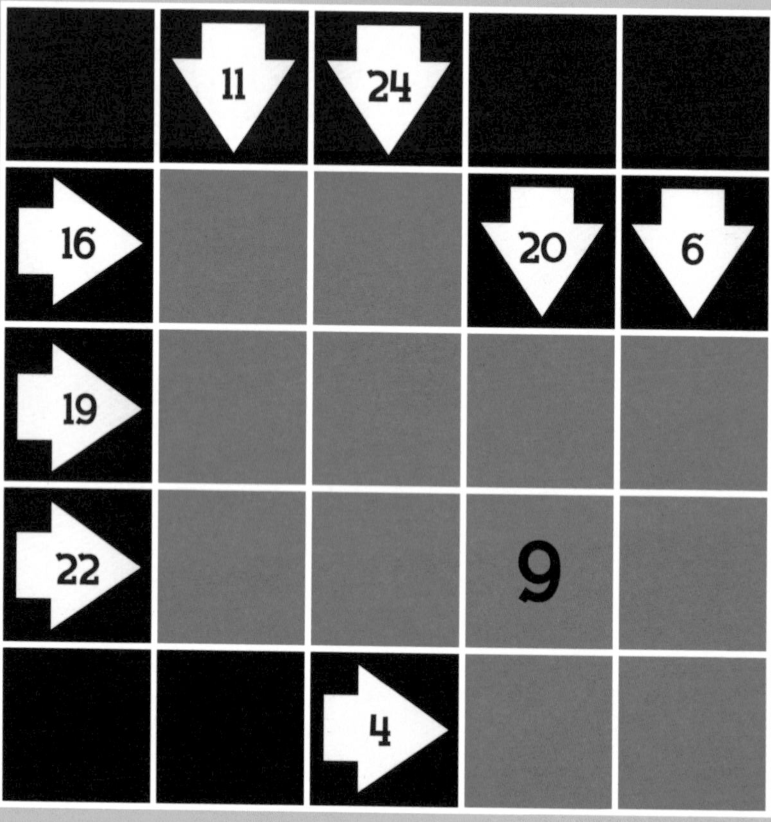

Desert trek

Circle the six things below that an explorer would find useful on a daytime trek across a hot, dry desert.

Vehicles quiz

1. A 'boneshaker' was an early form of which vehicle?

a) motorcar b) bicycle c) train

2. In a book by Roald Dahl, what did James fly all the way from England to New York: a big apple **or** a giant peach?

3. What are 'ships of the desert'?

a) jeeps b) hovercraft c) camels

4. What is the name of the vehicle that Scooby Doo and his gang travel around in?

a) The Mystery Machine

b) The Turbo Terrific

c) Chitty-Chitty-Bang-Bang

5. Which boats are paddled through the canals of Venice?

a) dinghies b) gondolas c) canoes

6. In the *Harry Potter* books, how was baby Harry delivered to his aunt and uncle's house?

a) broomstick b) flying carpet c) flying motorcycle

Doodle boats

Doodle on the shapes below to turn them into boats.

Busy road

Doodle lots of different vehicles on this busy road.

Souvenir mugs

These souvenir mugs are all for sale, but can you spot which one of them is the odd one out?

Memory story

 + A game for two or more people

1. One person begins a story by making up a short sentence and saying it out loud. It's best if the sentence is one that can easily be followed by another sentence.

2. The next person repeats the first sentence, then adds a sentence that follows on from the first in some way to continue the story.

TIP: It sometimes helps if you make your story a very weird and random one. Try to picture what's happening at each stage to help you remember, and listen carefully as each player retells it.

3. In each player's turn, they must tell the whole story so far from memory, before adding a new sentence at the end.

4. The game ends when someone forgets part of the story, or tells it in the wrong order.

One day, a hippo was having a swim. In fact he was at the best waterpark in town.

...best waterpark in town. He wanted to try out the huge new slide.

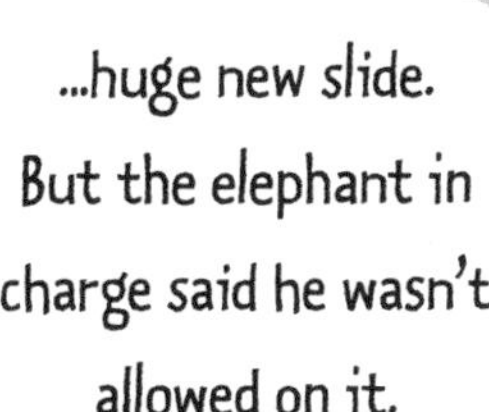

Rail code

Can you decipher the rail code? Read how the code works, then see if you can decipher the names of the five famous trains written below.

Rail code instructions

Every pair of letters in the concealed message is written one above the other, until the message is in two lines, like train tracks. So, 'The Mallard' is written: T E A L R
H M L A D

To make the code harder to crack, the two lines are written next to each other: T E A L R H M L A D

1. S E E S N R C E T V N O S O K T

2. T E R E T X R S H O I N E P E S

3. F Y N S O S A L I G C T M N

4. T E L E R I H B U T A N

5. T A S I E I N X R S R N S B R A E P E S

Safari adventure

Draw what you might see from your jeep while on safari.

Icy expedition

Which route should this polar explorer take to get back to his camp?

Vehicle find-it

Find all of the vehicles below hidden in the grid. Their names may be written in any direction.

YACHT	CANOE	PLANE	HOVERCRAFT
SUBMARINE	TRAIN	TRUCK	SLEIGH
FERRY	GONDOLA	BUS	BICYCLE

I A R T U Y S R E F Y G
C B U S H T P N I A R T
A E B R E C A N O E H F
N N L S L N S L O C G A
Y I C C D A A T Y A I R
F R Y A Y E H L M I E C
E A A O H C P A P R L R
R M P B A G I M A R S E
R B A Y H T O B C R O V
Y U N A C Y C L N Y E O
N S E A L O D N O G S H
A T K C U R T Y A P A N

Half ship

Finish the ship by drawing the mirror image of this half.

Hidden picture

Fill in the shapes that have blue dots. What can you see?

Missing symbols

Fill in the missing symbols to make each line true. Use < for "is less than," > for "is more than," and = for "is equal to."

The height of the Empire State Building  The height of the Eiffel Tower

The number of minutes in an hour  The number of seconds in a minute

The distance from London to Paris  The distance from Moscow to Tokyo

The number of seas there are said to be  The number of continents there are

The temperature at the North Pole  The temperature at the South Pole

The speed of sound  The speed of light

Car grid

In the grid below, draw squares around the groups of cars that match the groups shown on the right.

Cruise maze

See how quickly you can lead this cruise ship to the port.

Crossword 2

Use the clues below to fill in the correct words in the grid.

Across

1. Outdoor meal (6)
4. A green light means this (2)
5. Move quickly on your feet (3)
6. Opposite of late (5)
8. It goes with pepper (4)
11. Come last (4)
13. A guided journey (4)
14. The Sun is one (4)
16. A unicycle has one of these (5)
17. Burned remains (3)

Down

1. Locations for 1 across? (5)
2. Man-made waterway (5)
3. Frozen water (3)
4. Strong winds (5)
7. Shafts for 16 across (5)
9. In the past (3)
10. Number of blind mice (5)
12. Our planet (5)
13. Pull another vehicle (3)
15. Hot drink (3)

On the bus

Doodle faces on all the bus passengers.

End to end

\+ A game for two or more people

1. One person says a word, such as 'apple', or any other word they can think of.

2. Someone else has to say another word that starts with the last letter of the word that's just been said. In this example, they could say 'elephant' or 'extraordinary' or any other word that has 'e' as the first letter.

3. Everyone takes turns to say a word that starts with the last letter of the previous word. The game continues as long as everyone wants to play.

Another idea: If you want to make the game harder, then before you start, you could all agree just to use words from one category, such as animals or countries.

Truck parts

Circle the group of parts that can be put together to make the truck shown on the right.

A

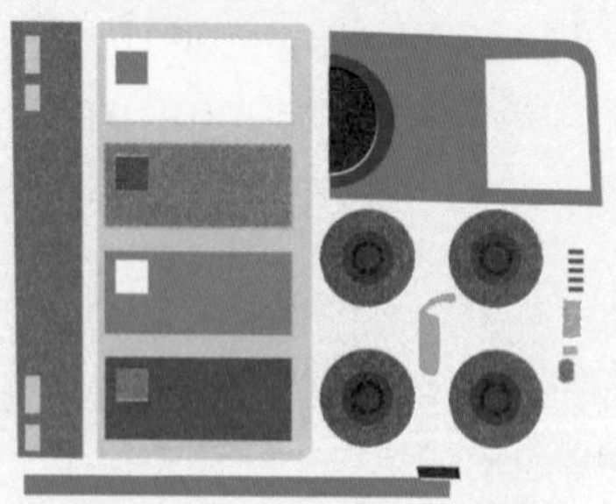

B

C

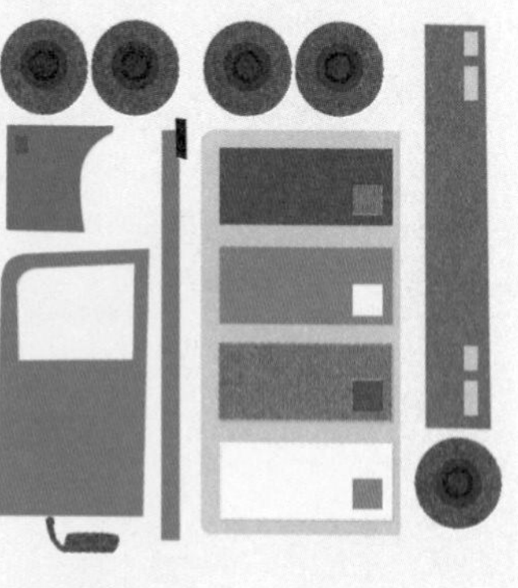

D

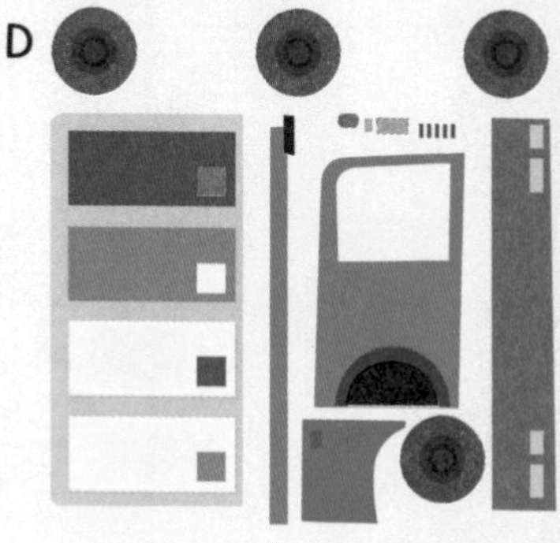

E

F

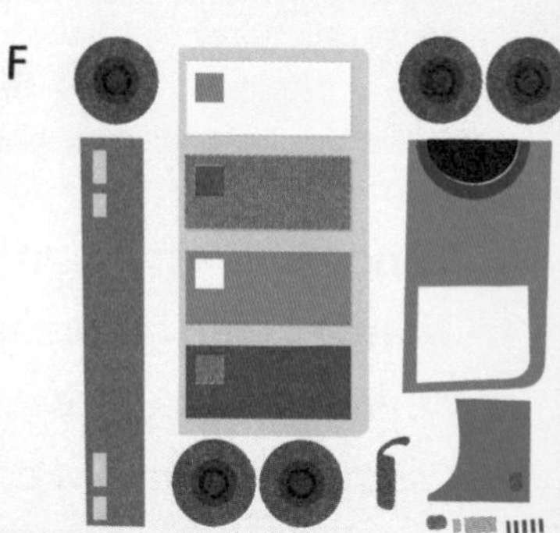

Sudoku

The grid is made up of nine blocks, each containing nine squares. Fill in the blank squares so that each block, row and column contains all the digits 1 to 9.

1	5	9	7		2			6
		6		1				4
	4	3			5	7		
			4	2	6	1		
9				7				5
		4	5	9	8		7	
		8	9				6	
4				5	7			
		7	6			5	2	1

Quickest route

Jamie, Evie and Ryan all live in La Plane, and know all the shortcuts they can take through the town at certain times.

OPENING TIMES

Park: 9am–5pm Market: 9am–7pm

School: 8am–7pm Supermarket: 9am–5pm

(Gates are locked at all other times)

Look at the opening times given on the sign above, and use the information to help you draw the quickest route on the map on the right for the following journeys:

1. Evie from home to the pool at 4pm.

2. Jamie from home to school at 9:30am.

3. Ryan from the pool to Big D's Diner at 6:30pm.

4. Evie from the library to the pool at 5:30pm.

5. Jamie from the library to Big D's Diner at 6:45pm.

6. Ryan from home to Jamie's house at 4:30pm.

Jamie lives here
Evie lives here
Park
Big D's
Pool
School
Supermarket
Market
Ryan lives here
Library
Key:
Wall
Gate

Symmetry

On the grids below, the dotted lines are mirrors. Draw the reflection of each shape in the correct place on the other half of its grid.

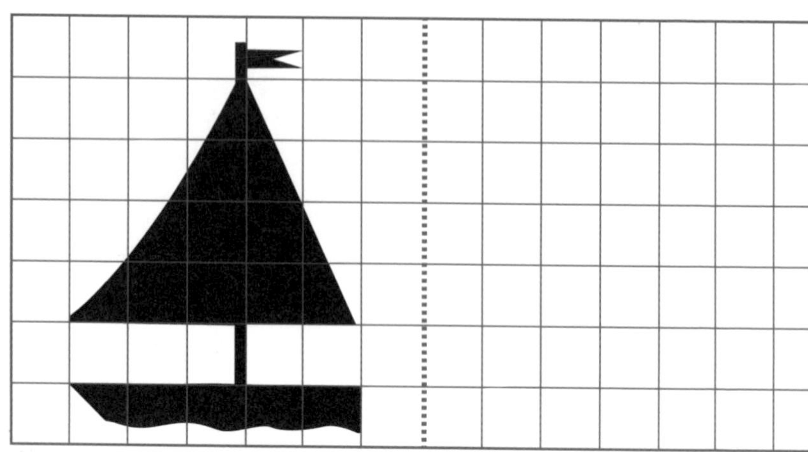

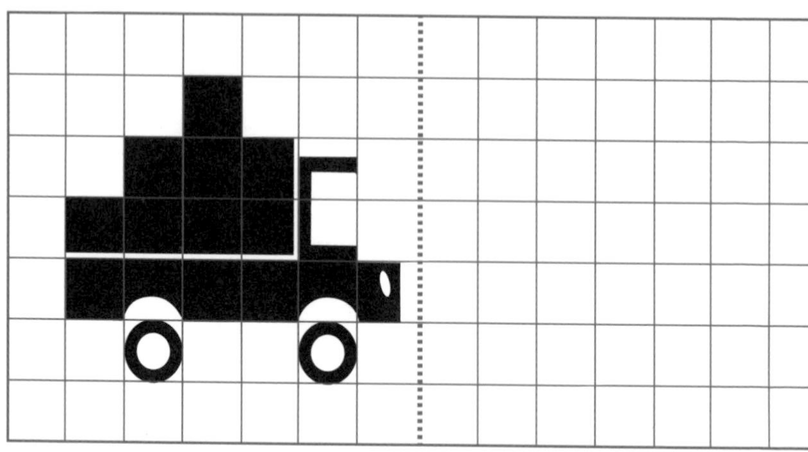

Hot-air race

Five hot-air balloons were in a race. *Monsoon* wasn't first, but finished two places in front of *Topper*. *Emerald* finished before *Sunbeam* but after *Duskrider*. No balloon with red stripes finished last. Write the correct finishing position on each balloon's basket.

Doodle cars

Doodle bright patterns on these vehicles.

Compass points

Use the compass directions at the bottom to find the correct locations for the missing letters. When you have filled in all the letters, see if you can discover the hidden names of four well-known rivers.

A	D	S	I	D	Y		
C	M	S	E	L	T		
....	Y	....	O	....	N	O	C
I	T	M	....	N	N	R	Y
....	A	R	S	O	I	A	K
E	V	M	A	B	....	P	....

Write a **G** in a space that is South of an L.
Write an **L** in a space that is North of an E.
Write a **Z** in a space that is East of an M.
Write an **N** in a space that is West of a P.
Write an **A** in a space that is East of a Y.
Write a **G** in a space that is South of a K.
Write an **N** in a space that is North of an I.

Camping gear

How many **different** camping objects can you count in the jumble below? How many objects are there altogether?

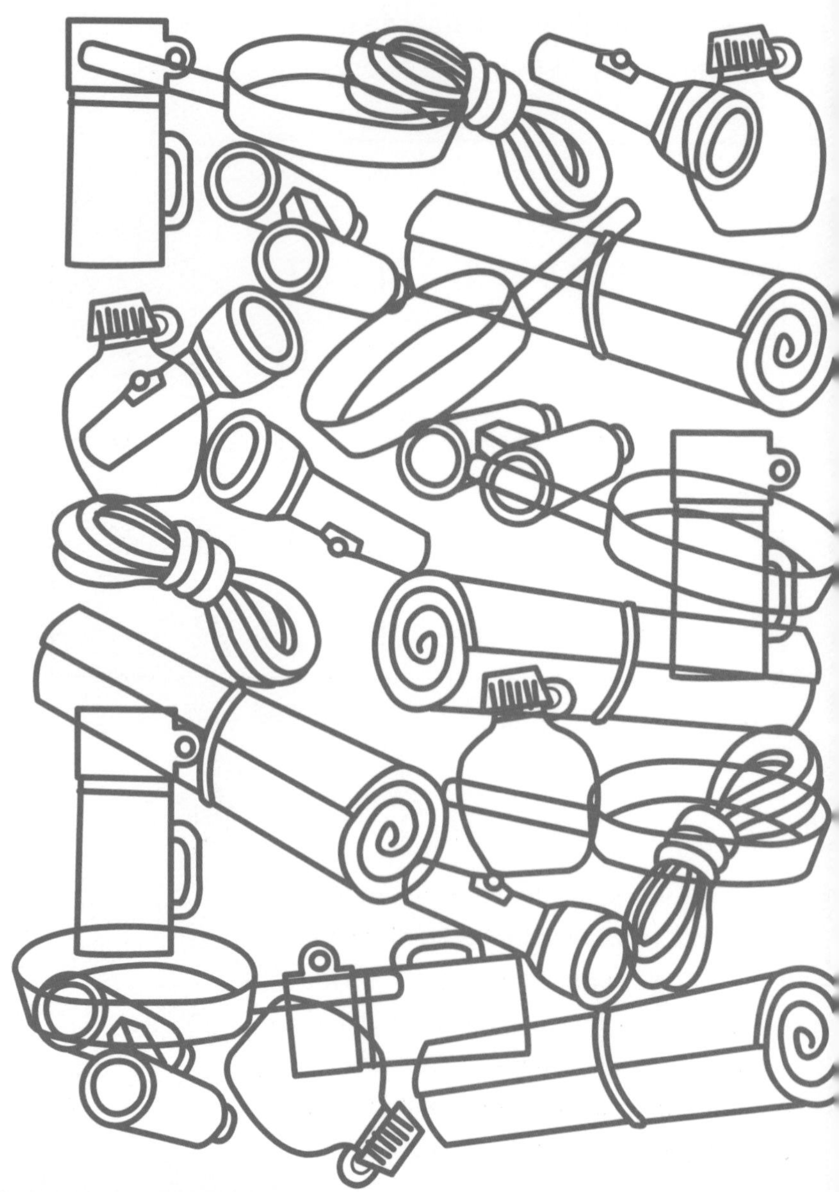

Crocodile crossing

Draw a path across this jungle river, landing only on logs, and avoiding the crocodiles.

Hidden destinations

Can you find these travel words hidden in the sentences below? The first one has been done for you.

FARM ZOO MUSEUM

~~PARK~~ CONCERT

BEACH

CASTLE PICNIC

1. The navy named the new shi**p 'Ark**ansas'.
2. You'll be a champion one day.
3. If there's a storm, use umbrellas.
4. Turning the music on certainly helped.
5. The weather forecast let us down.
6. The scary monster had lots of arms.
7. I think she handled the topic nicely.
8. The camera zoomed in on the boy.

Draw a hot-air balloon

Follow the steps below to draw a hot-air balloon, then fill the sky with lots more of them.

1. Draw this shape for the balloon.

2. Add these lines and a basket.

3. Draw these lines for ropes.

True or false?

For each of the statements below, circle 'T' if you think it's true, or 'F' if you think it's false.

1. When Christopher Columbus discovered North America, he actually thought he'd landed in India. **T / F**

2. The long-distance races called marathons are named after the site of a battle in Ancient Greece. **T / F**

3. Eskimos have over 50 words for snow. **T / F**

4. The Antarctic is the driest desert on Earth. **T / F**

5. South of the Equator, water spirals down a drain in the opposite direction from north of the Equator. **T / F**

6. A homing pigeon can be used to take messages back and forth between two places. **T / F**

7. The Spanish national anthem has no words. **T / F**

8. Sydney is the capital of Australia. **T / F**

Baggage claim

Dori has to collect her suitcase from the baggage claim. Find her a route through the maze below.

Fantastic houses

Turn these rectangles into four fantastic houses.

Continental search

Link each country at the bottom with the continent that it is in, then find all of them hidden in the grid. Their names may be written in any direction.

Africa Europe Egypt Chile

Asia North America Fiji Oceania

Sweden Japan Canada South America

Plane, wing, bird

 + A game for two or more people

1. To start, someone chooses a word, then says it out loud. For example, you could say 'plane' as the first word.

2. Someone else then says a word they associate with the first word. For instance, the word 'plane' might make them think of the word 'wing' in this example.

3. The next person says a word that they associate with the word that has just been said. After 'wing' the next person might say 'bird' or 'bee' or something else that flies. That might lead on to 'feather' or 'buzz' or 'flower' and so on.

4. The game continues with everyone taking turns to say a word. If anyone pauses, or repeats a word that's already been said, they lose, and the game starts again with a new word.

Cycling maze

Guide the cyclist up a clear trail to the top of the mountain.

Morse code message

The captain has just received this urgent message in Morse code from another ship in the area. Use the key to decode the message, and write it below. Each letter is separated by a slash.

Key:

A . _
B _ . . .
C _ . _ .
D _ . .
E .
F . . _ .
G _ _ .
H . . . .
I . .
J . _ _ _
K _ . _
L . _ . .
M _ _
N _ .
O _ _ _
P . _ _ .
Q _ _ . _
R . _ .
S . . .
T _
U . . _
V . . . _
W . _ _
X _ . . _
Y _ . _ _
Z _ _ . .

_ . . . / . / . _ _ / . _ /
. _ . / . / . . / _ . _ .
. / _ . . . / . / . _ . /
_ _ . / . . . / . _ /
. . . . / . / . _ / _ . .

Official Translation Pap

Bigger boat

Draw another boat on the grid, exactly the same shape but twice as big. The first part has been done for you.

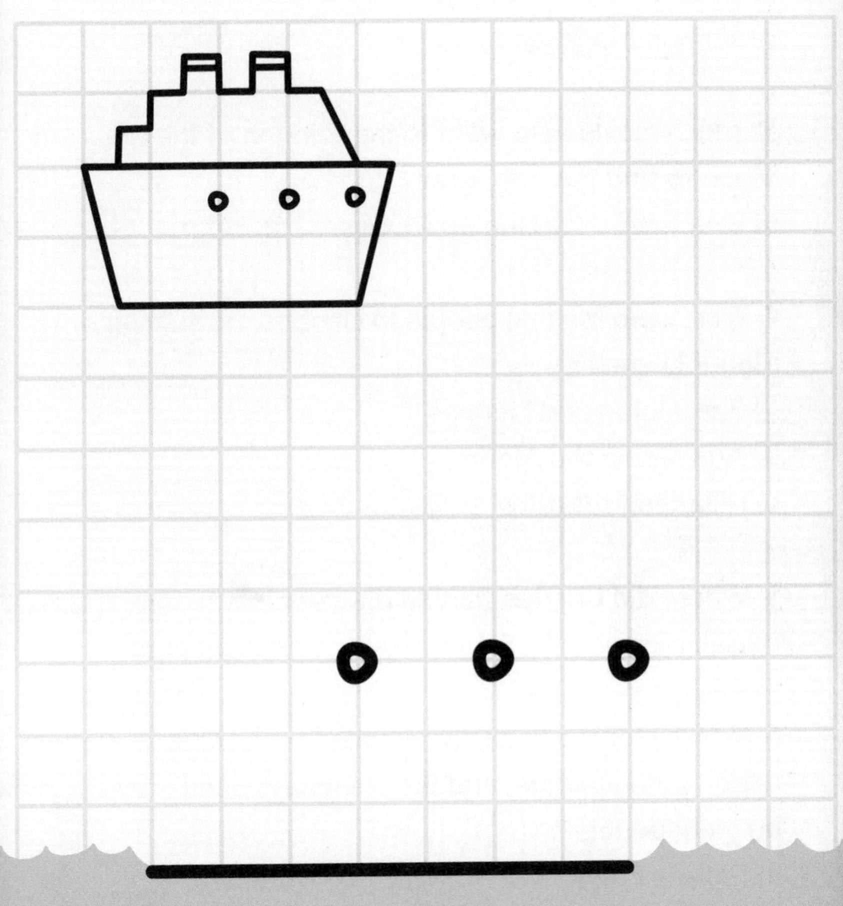

Expeditions quiz

1. Which was the first mission to take astronauts to the Moon?

a) Apollo 1 b) Apollo 11 c) Apollo 13

2. Who led the first expedition to sail around the world, but died along the way: Christopher Columbus **or** Ferdinand Magellan?

3. Which movie hero went to the Canyon of the Crescent Moon to find the Holy Grail?

a) Lara Croft b) Indiana Jones c) Tintin

4. Who were the first people to climb to the summit of Mount Everest?

a) Shackleton and Fiennes

b) Armstrong and Aldrin

c) Hillary and Tenzing

5. Where did Charles Darwin discover lots of new species?

a) Galápagos b) Seychelles c) Philippines

6. Which storybook explorer visited both Lilliput, ruled by tiny people, and Brobdingnag, ruled by giant people?

a) Phileas Fogg

b) Willy Wonka

c) Gulliver

66

Bridge words

Find a word that can go after the word on the left and in front of the word on the right to make two new words.

Suitcase designs

Doodle some designs on your suitcases so you can spot them easily.

Troubling trains

1. Trains travel from Rivertown to Ashville all day, always on the same track, always going nonstop and at the same speed. The noon train took 80 minutes to complete the trip, but the 4pm train took an hour and 20 minutes. Can you explain how this is possible?

2. Two trains enter the same single-track tunnel from opposite ends at exactly seven o'clock, then appear again just five minutes later, totally undamaged. Think carefully about how this could happen.

3. A train is going from Gladestone to Sapphire City, stopping at Streamside and Milltown. At Gladestone, 88 passengers are on the train. Some people get off at Streamside, and 12 get on. At Milltown, 45 people get on and 12 get off. When it reaches Sapphire City, there are 120 passengers on the train. How many people got off at Streamside?

Train tracks

Doodle a winding track for the train to follow.

Crossword 3

Use the clues below to fill in the correct words in the grid.

Across

1. Where boats arrive (4)
3. A large boat (4)
7. Not asleep (5)
8. In front (5)
10. Quick, rapid (4)
11. Speed contest (4)
12. Kingdom (5)
15. Come to a halt (4)
16. Lacking moisture (3)

Down

1. Where a train pulls up (8)
2. What cars travel on (5)
4. One lost an 11 across to a tortoise (4)
5. Small lake (4)
6. Large area of salt water (3)
9. What keeps a boat in place (6)
13. Social insect (3)
14. It shows you the way (3)

Hidden picture

Fill in the shapes that have pink dots. What can you see?

Quick-fire ten

A game for two people

1. One person thinks of a category of things, such as countries, famous people, vehicles, animals or kinds of food.

2. The other person has to think of ten things in that category in one minute. If they succeed, they get one point.

TIP: Some categories are easier than others – for example, 'animals' is easy because there are lots of kinds of animals. If you want to make a game harder, choose a category such as 'water sports' or 'cartoon animals' that has fewer things in it.

3. Take turns to be the one to think of the category. The first person to get to five points is the winner.

Food!

Landing trail

Find out where this plane is touching down.

Sail patterns

Doodle lots of different patterns on the sails of these yachts.

East by east

How many times can you find the word EAST in the grid below? It may be written in any direction.

S T E A S T A
T E A S E A S E T
T S A E A E T T A S T
T A A S A S E T S E E
S E T S A E A S A T S
A S T E E T S A E T A
E T A S T A T E T S T
A E S T A A S E A A E
A T A S E A T S E
E S E A T S E

A walk in the woods

Help Little Red Riding Hood reach Granny's cottage along the shortest route. She can only walk across clearings where the answer is an even number.

Spot the difference

Can you spot the ten differences between these two buses going on a trip?

Cloud doodles

Turn these clouds into all sorts of creatures.

Rural express

Guide the train along the right track to the station.

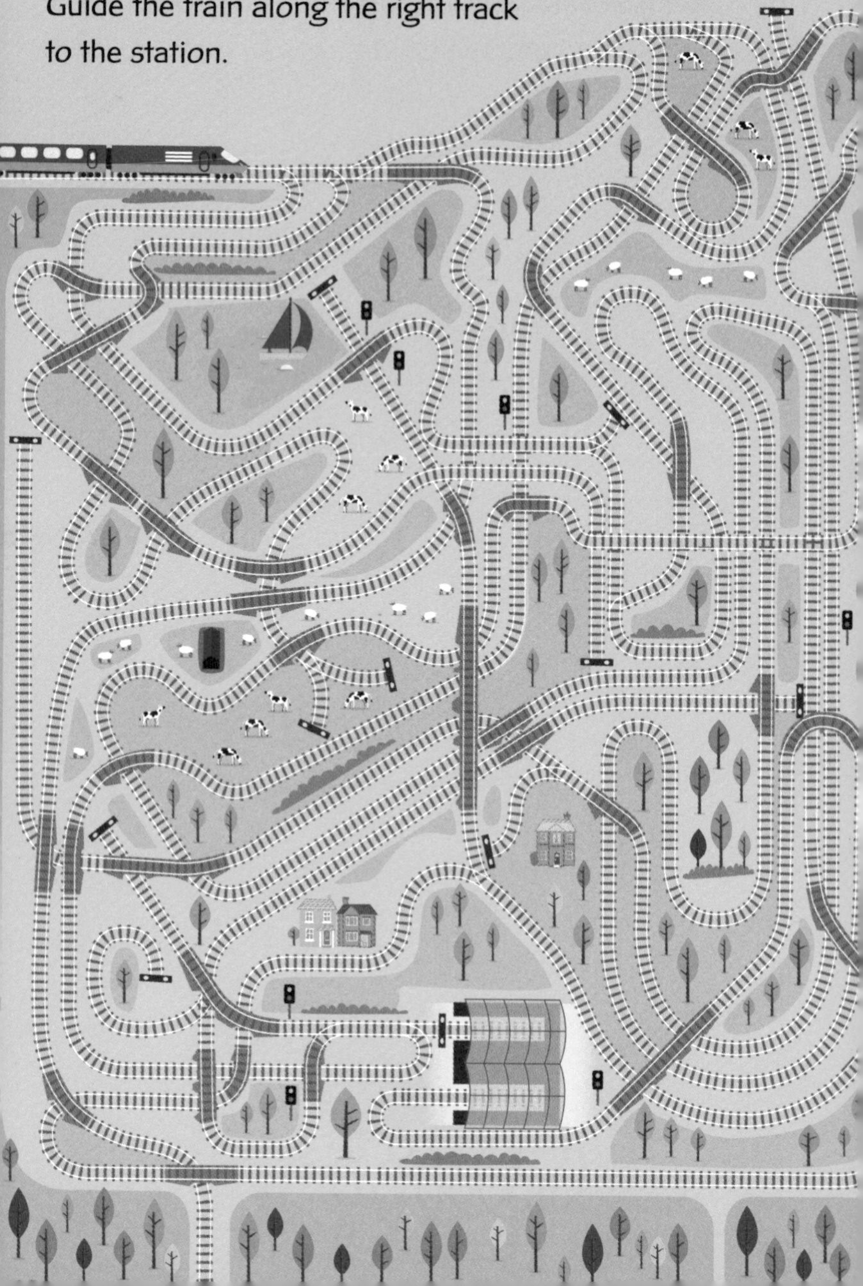

From above

A helicopter is hovering over an area of the city. Looking at the pilot's view, can you see which group of buildings he is directly above?

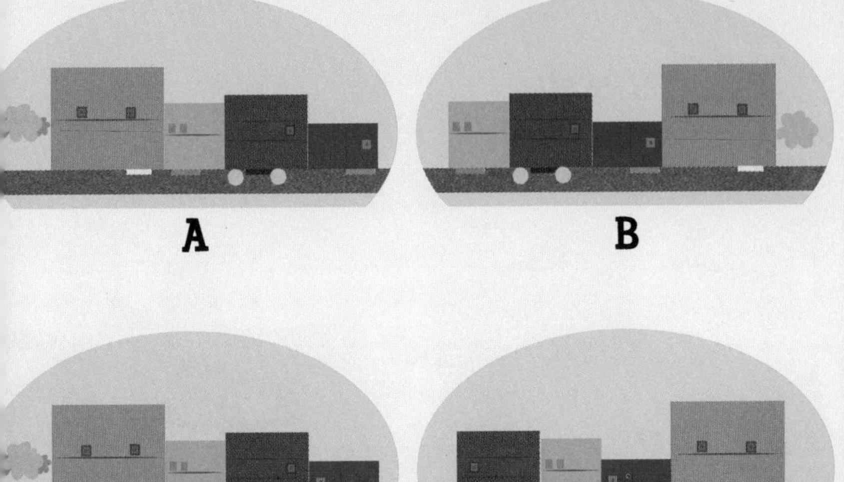

Doodle planes

Doodle bright patterns on these planes.

Shipping scramble

Can you unscramble these letters to find the names of six things you might find on a ship?

1. drured
2. lerlopper
3. hornac
4. stifr team
5. hopotrel
6. nunelf

Oh no! But...

 + A game for two or more people

1. Someone starts the game by saying a sentence that begins 'Oh no...' then finishes it by saying something bad. For example, 'Oh no, there is a monster coming our way!'

2. Someone else replies with a sentence that begins 'But...' followed by something that stops the situation from being bad. In this example, you could say, 'But he doesn't have any teeth.'

3. The game continues with everyone taking turns to add sentences that start with 'But...' that take the situation from bad to good and back again. For example, 'But he's breathing fire.' 'But I have a hose.' 'But it doesn't work.' And so on.

4. The game ends when someone can't think of anything to add to what the last person has said.

Camping conundrum

Can you find a place to pitch your tent? In the squares immediately around it (up, down, left, right and diagonally) it must have three trees, *one* campfire, and *no* wolves. Draw a tent in the correct square.

Motor race

Help the car race through this maze in record time.

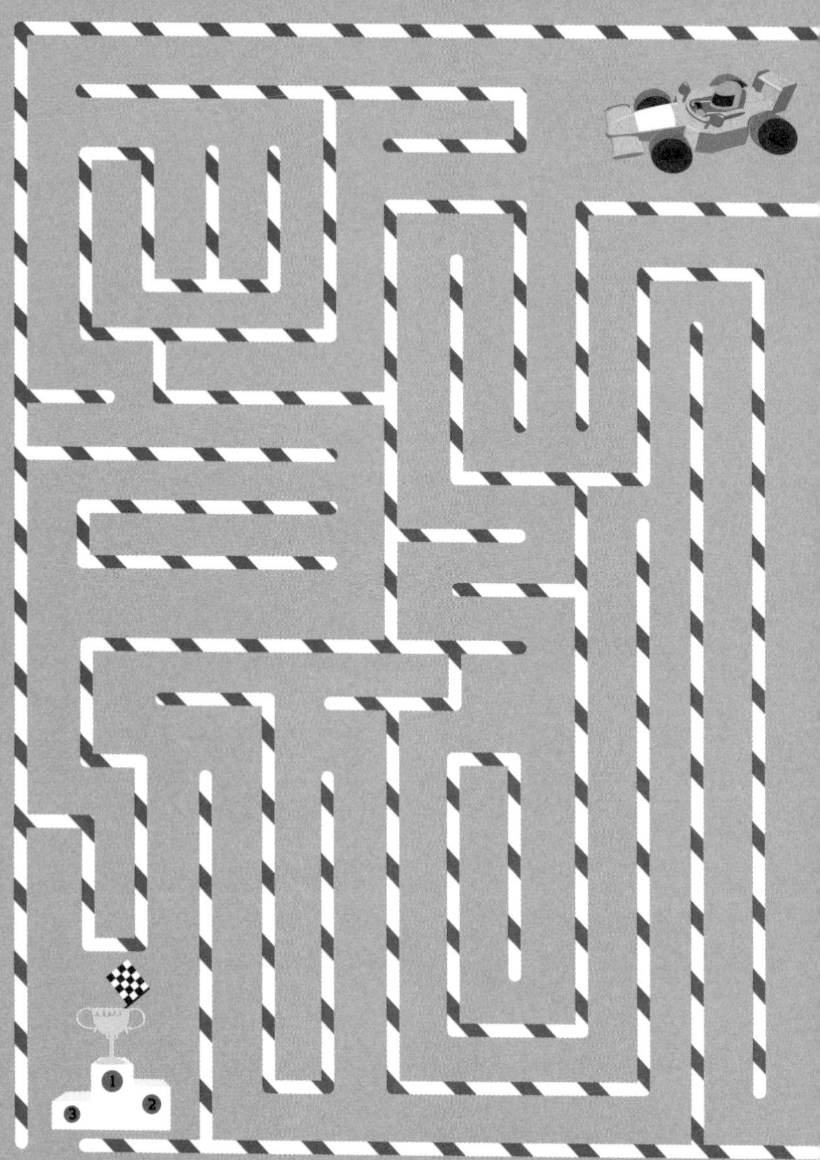

Sail the seas quiz

1. Where was the *Titanic* sailing to when it sank?

a) Cape Town b) New York c) Southampton

2. Which storybook character was shipwrecked on a Caribbean island?

a) Robinson Crusoe b) Don Quixote c) Peter Pan

3. The speedy ships that sailed between Europe and China in the mid-nineteenth century were known as what?

a) coffee cutters b) tea clippers c) sugar sloops

4. Which ghost ship was said to be condemned to sail the seas for all eternity?

a) *Mary Celeste*
b) *The Dawn Treader*
c) *The Flying Dutchman*

5. What nickname do sailors traditionally use for the bottom of the sea: The Captain's Graveyard **or** Davy Jones's Locker?

6. Which area of the Atlantic Ocean are ships said to have sailed into and never been seen again?

a) Bermuda Triangle
b) Jamaica Circle
c) Haiti Square

Off course

These yachts have been blown off course. Which ones will find their way to the docks?

Passport photo

Draw a face and some hair on this passport photo.

Draw a train

Follow the steps below to draw a steam train, then fill the page with lots more of them.

1. Draw wheels and a base.

2. Add these shapes on top.

3. Draw a funn and final detai

90

Cycle routes

Three friends leave their homes at the same time and cycle to the lake, taking different routes. Circle the cyclist who will reach the lake first if...

...**Adam** cycles up and down one hill every ten minutes, but he has to go back home for his sandwiches, which adds 25 minutes to his time.

...**Sunil** cycles up and down one hill every 11 minutes, but spends ten minutes fixing a puncture.

...**Lance** cycles up and down one hill every 12 minutes, and he rides to the lake without stopping.

91

Lost in the fog

The outlines of two of the boats below are visible through the fog. Can you circle which ones they are?

Shipping search

Find all of the famous ships below hidden in the grid. Their names may be written in any direction.

TITANIC	LUSITANIA	GOLDEN HIND	DISCOVERY
VICTORY	BOUNTY	BEAGLE	POTEMKIN
CUTTY SARK	MAYFLOWER	MARY ROSE	BISMARCK

I	C	R	L	U	Y	P	R	V	L	O	G
L	K	Y	R	E	V	O	C	S	I	D	T
U	R	V	Y	G	L	N	L	I	E	N	C
S	A	M	S	P	O	T	E	M	K	I	N
I	S	A	C	D	B	A	T	Y	N	H	K
T	Y	Y	T	N	U	O	B	A	I	N	C
A	T	F	R	H	C	E	T	D	R	E	R
N	T	L	B	O	A	I	M	A	Y	D	A
I	U	O	Y	G	T	O	B	C	R	L	M
A	C	W	L	P	Y	C	L	N	Y	O	S
N	S	E	A	L	O	D	I	A	G	G	I
M	A	R	Y	R	O	S	E	V	U	O	B

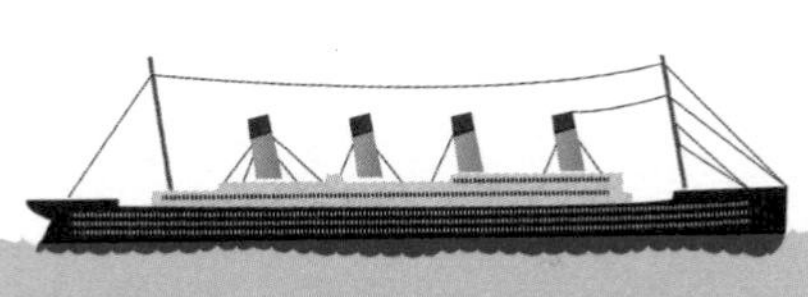

93

Hidden picture

Fill in the shapes that have green dots. What can you see?

Logical lines

1. Circle the plane behind the plane that's two behind the plane that's in front of the blue plane.

2. Circle the helicopter two in front of the one that's in front of the one that's two behind the green helicopter.

3. Circle the car in front of the car that's two behind the car that's behind the orange car.

Busy campsite

Draw lots more tents in this campsite.

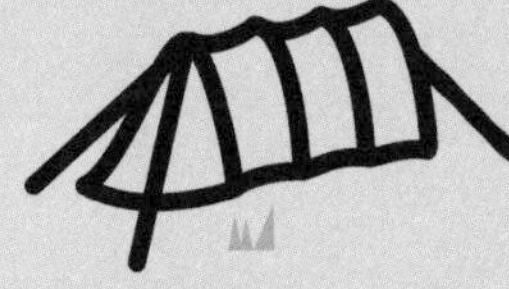

SeeKing explorers

Find the names of all the famous explorers at the bottom hidden in the grid. Their names may be written in any direction.

C	N	E	S	D	N	U	M	A	O	N	B	R	R	D
F	O	P	N	I	D	E	P	O	L	O	R	E	M	L
P	I	Z	A	R	D	I	A	R	I	S	B	I	V	Y
M	L	H	N	I	W	A	S	D	U	C	P	T	W	N
R	A	V	D	R	L	B	M	B	E	I	X	R	T	A
M	T	O	B	A	C	R	M	G	Z	R	S	A	I	M
A	I	P	A	K	O	U	O	A	U	E	T	C	Z	A
G	U	A	C	G	L	R	R	B	W	A	R	B	R	G
E	H	C	U	O	Y	R	C	T	D	A	L	B	D	A
L	U	V	C	L	O	L	M	O	S	R	L	T	U	D
L	O	G	L	A	T	K	P	S	R	C	A	L	B	I
A	R	O	D	W	N	Y	E	J	O	T	N	K	L	D
N	V	I	L	P	I	C	C	U	P	S	E	V	E	S
O	A	H	B	Z	V	P	E	S	N	H	F	S	N	W
S	L	U	E	R	I	C	S	R	E	K	B	H	F	N

Amundsen
Magellan
Cook
Vespucci
Polo
Columbus
Ericson
Dias
Drake
Pizarro
Cabot
Cartier
Cortes
da Gama

Draw a boat

Follow the steps below to draw a boat, then fill the sea with lots more of them.

1. Draw this shape for the boat.

2. Add a mast and a sail.

3. Draw another sail and a flag.

Journey quiz

1. Who marched over the Alps with elephants in his army to attack the Roman Empire?

a) Alexander the Great b) Attila the Hun c) Hannibal

2. What is the Swahili word for a journey?

a) trek b) walkabout c) safari

3. Which mythical creatures were said to lure sailors to their doom?

a) sirens b) banshees c) harpies

4. Whose face 'launched a thousand ships'?

a) Cleopatra b) Helen of Troy c) Aphrodite

5. What are mapmakers called?

a) cartographers b) orienteers c) geographers

6. In *The Lord of the Rings,* where were the hobbits Frodo and Sam trying to get to?

a) Isengard b) Mordor c) The Shire

7. Who "went to sea in a beautiful pea-green boat"?

a) Bobby Shafto

b) Sinbad the Sailor

c) The Owl and the Pussycat

Bus doodles

Turn the rectangles below into different buses.

To the lighthouse

Lead the boat through the choppy waters to the lighthouse ladder.

Answers

1. Signpost scramble:

1. LONDON 2. MADRID
3. NEW YORK 4. RIO DE JANEIRO
5. BERLIN 6. PARIS 7. MOSCOW
8. ROME 9. SYDNEY

2. Vehicle timeline:

1. Sailing ship 2. Submarine
3. Bicycle 4. Car 5. Plane
6. Hovercraft

4. Vehicle search:

12 vehicles

6. Safari search:

L	E	O	P	B	I	G	C	A	R	D	N
C	Z	A	L	L	I	R	O	G	E	E	A
D	C	D	R	B	P	I	P	R	Y	N	O
O	E	Z	H	A	T	E	E	H	C	L	C
H	F	C	E	I	R	Z	F	I	A	R	T
Y	F	Z	U	B	P	H	Y	P	O	D	N
E	A	A	N	U	R	P	M	C	N	A	A
N	R	O	B	F	O	A	O	T	I	S	H
A	I	R	Y	F	T	D	N	C	H	O	P
L	G	N	A	A	I	A	M	A	R	E	E
N	S	E	E	L	L	Z	E	T	D	S	L
A	Z	L	E	O	P	A	R	D	Y	A	E

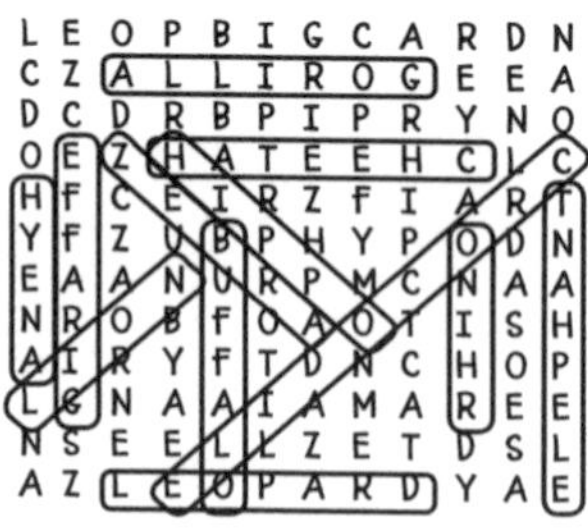

7. Helicopter match-up:

9. On safari:

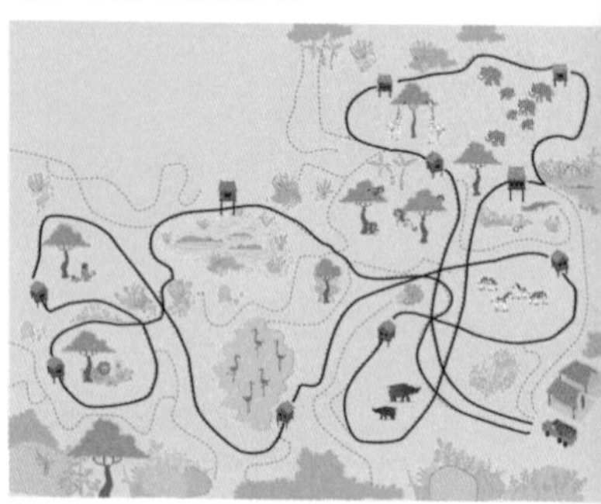

11. Voyage sudoku:

G	E	O	V	Y	A
A	V	Y	E	O	G
Y	O	A	G	V	E
O	G	E	Y	A	V
E	Y	V	A	G	O
V	A	G	O	E	Y

12. Tunnel traffic:

Fastest: 5 Slowest: 2

13. Transport trickery:

1. He was walking down the stre
2. His horse was called Friday.
3. Both are the same distance frc Dublin as they pass each other.

14. Hidden picture:

Answers

15. Spot the difference:

17. River route:

18. Crossword 1:

19. Timely inventions:

1. Wheel 2. Compass
3. Globe 4. Diesel engine
5. Radar 6. Satnav

20. Bridge crossing:

1 - Emma and Jon cross. (2 mins.)
2 - Jon comes back. (4 mins.)
3 - Isla and Marc cross. (14 mins.)
4 - Emma comes back. (15 mins.)
5 - Emma and Jon cross. (17 mins.)

22. Camping equipment:

P D C T U Y S R E F M G
C B I N O C U L A R S T
A E O T K C O N O S N F
N G A B G N I P E E L S
T I P C D A D T T S I S
E R Y A T E A L F S E A
E A T O M C R A G A L P
N M P E A O I M R L S M
K C A P K C A B C G O O
Y H N A C C C L N N E C
W S E D I O A N O U S U
E L T S I H W J A S A N

24. Dock deductions:

Thursday	Freedom	2	Jack
Friday	Skimmer	1	Pete
Saturday	Mermaid	3	Sam

26. Plane trails: A

27. Cross sum:

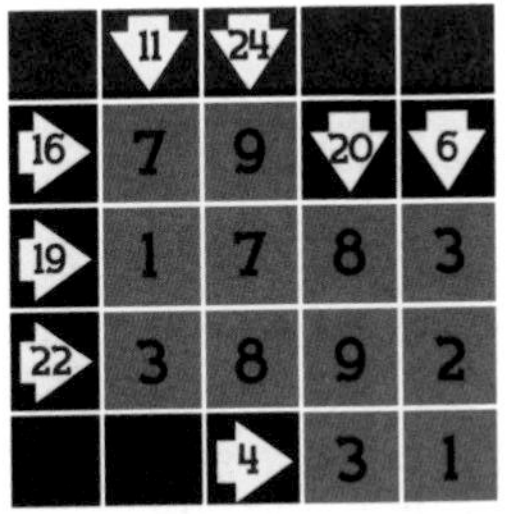

Answers

28. Desert trek:

29. Vehicles quiz:

1. b 2. giant peach
3. c 4. a 5. b 6. c

32. Souvenir mugs:

34. Rail code:

1. Stevenson's Rocket
2. The Orient Express
3. Flying Scotsman
4. The Blue Train
5. Trans Siberian Express

36. Icy expedition: c

37. Vehicle find-it:

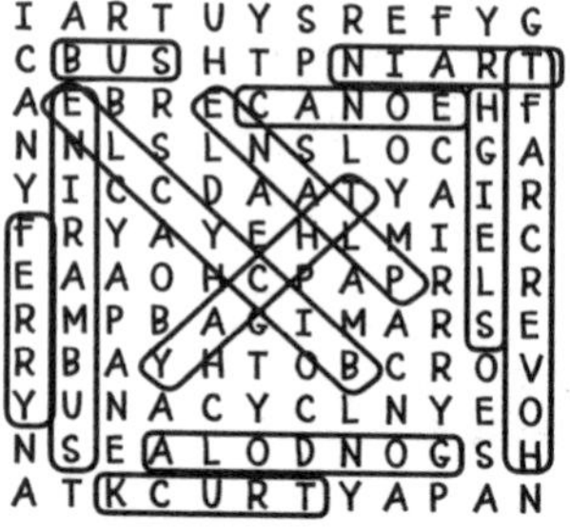

39. Hidden picture:

40. Missing symbols:

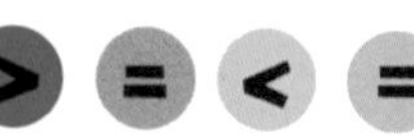

41. Car grid:

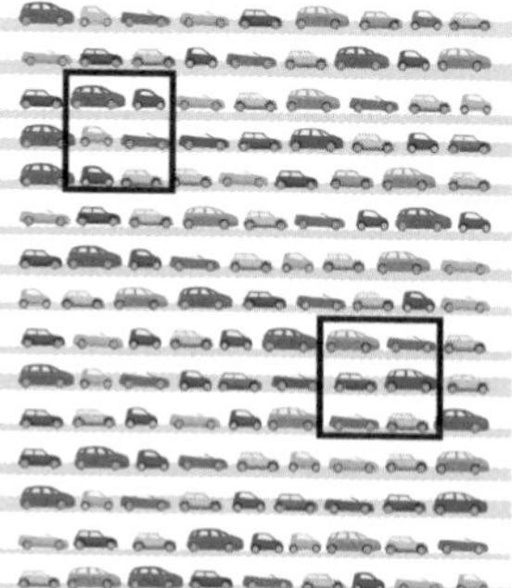

42. Cruise maze:

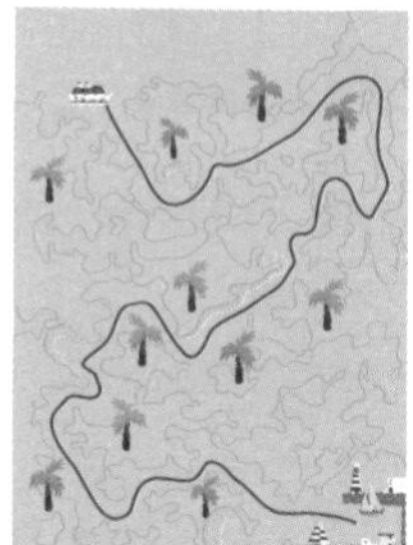

Answers

43. Crossword 2:

p	i	c	n	i	c		g	o
a		a		c			a	
r	u	n		e	a	r	l	y
k		a			x		e	
s	a	l	t		l	o	s	e
	g		h		e			a
t	o	u	r		s	t	a	r
o			e			e		t
w	h	e	e	l		a	s	h

46. Truck parts: E

47. Sudoku:

1	5	9	7	4	2	8	3	6
8	7	6	3	1	9	2	5	4
2	4	3	8	6	5	7	1	9
7	3	5	4	2	6	1	9	8
9	8	2	1	7	3	6	4	5
6	1	4	5	9	8	3	7	2
5	2	8	9	3	1	4	6	7
4	6	1	2	5	7	9	8	3
3	9	7	6	8	4	5	2	1

48. Quickest route:

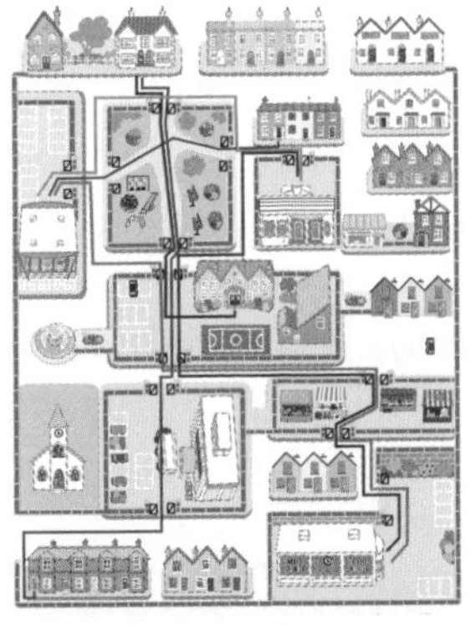

49. Symmetry:

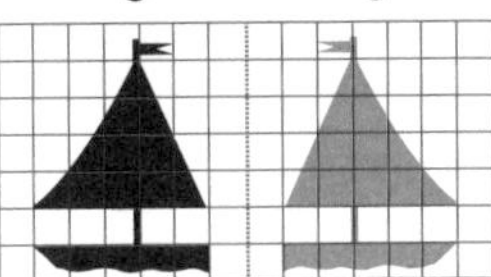

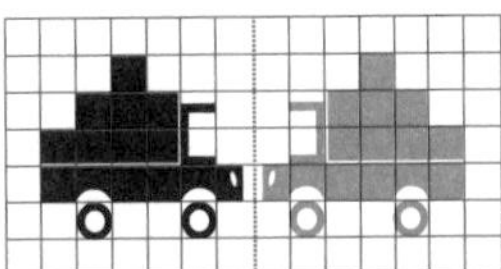

50. Hot-air race:

1. *Duskrider* 2. *Emerald*
3. *Monsoon* 4. *Sunbeam*
5. *Topper*

52. Compass points:

53. Camping gear:

7 different objects, 27 altogether

54. Crocodile crossing:

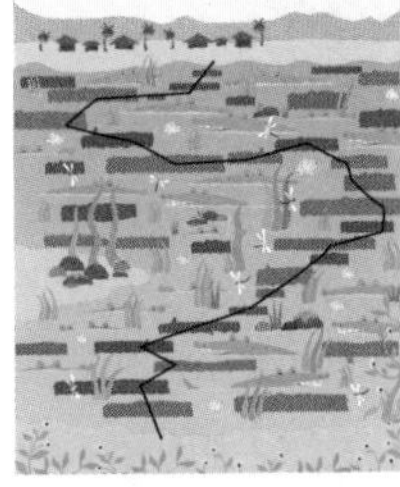

Answers

55. Hidden destinations:

1. The navy named the new shi**p 'Ark**ansas'.
2. You'll **be a ch**ampion one day.
3. If there's a stor**m, use um**brellas.
4. Turning the musi**c on cert**ainly helped.
5. The weather fore**cast le**t us down.
6. The scary monster had lots o**f arms**.
7. I think she handled the to**pic nic**ely.
8. The camera **zoo**med in on the boy.

57. True or false?:

1. True 2. True 3. False 4. True
5. False 6. False 7. True 8. False

58. Baggage claim:

60. Continental search:

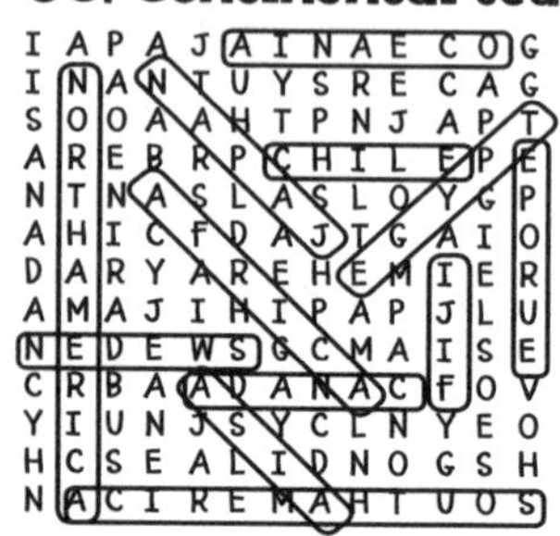

Canada - North America,
Chile - South America,
Egypt - Africa, Fiji - Oceania,
Japan - Asia, Sweden - Europe

62. Cycling maze:

63. Morse code message:

BEWARE ICEBERGS AHEAD

64. Bigger boat:

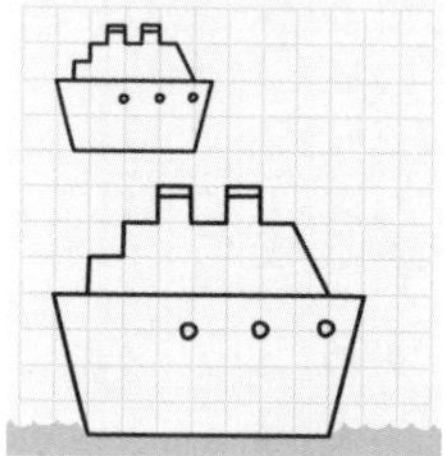

65. Expeditions quiz:

1. b 2. Ferdinand Magellan
3. b 4. c 5. a 6. c

66. Bridge words:

1. night 2. watch 3. wood
4. book 5. table 6. fish 7. toe

68. Troubling trains:

1. 80 minutes is the same as an hour and 20 minutes.
2. They enter at 7 a.m. and 7 p.m.
3. 13 people

Answers

70. Crossword 3:

71. Hidden picture:

73. Landing trail:

San Francisco

75. East by east: 15

76. A walk in the woods:

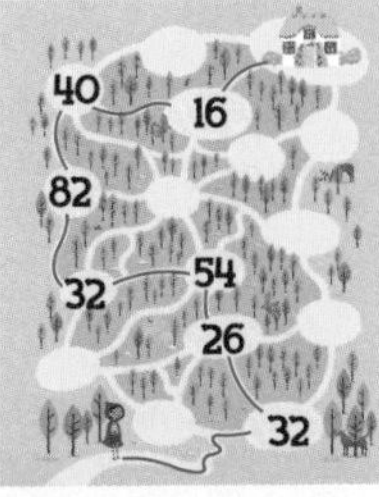

77. Spot the difference:

79. Rural express:

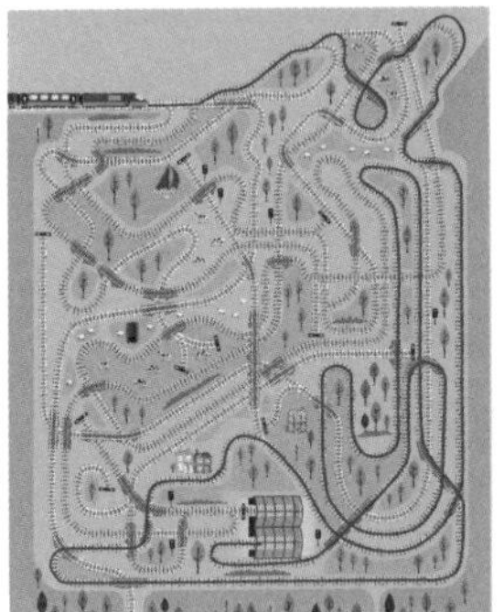

80. From above: A

82. Shipping scramble:

1. rudder 2. propeller 3. anchor
4. first mate 5. porthole 6. funnel

84. Camping conundrum:

Answers

85. Motor race:

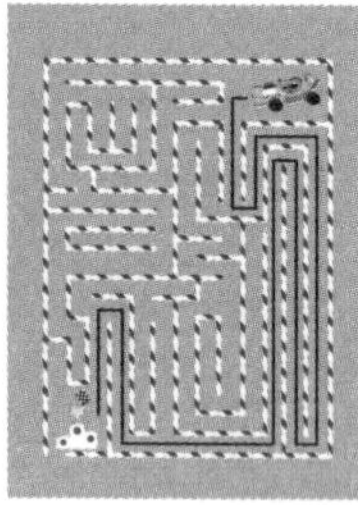

86. Sail the seas quiz:

1. b 2. a 3. b 4. c 5. Davy Jones's Locker 6. a

87. Off course: A and D

90. Cycle routes:

Sunil reaches the lake first.

91. Lost in the fog:

92. Shipping search:

I	C	R	L	U	Y	P	R	V	L	O	G
L	K	Y	R	E	V	O	C	S	I	D	T
U	R	V	Y	G	L	N	L	I	E	N	C
S	A	M	S	P	O	T	E	M	K	I	N
I	S	A	C	D	B	A	T	Y	N	H	K
T	Y	Y	T	N	U	O	B	A	I	N	C
A	T	F	R	H	C	E	T	D	R	E	R
N	T	L	B	O	A	I	M	A	Y	D	A
I	U	O	Y	G	T	O	B	C	R	L	M
A	C	W	L	P	Y	C	L	N	Y	O	S
N	S	E	A	L	O	D	I	A	G	G	I
M	A	R	Y	R	O	S	E	V	U	O	B

93. Hidden picture:

94. Logical lines:

1. green 2. yellow 3. red

96. Seeking explorers:

C	N	E	S	D	N	U	M	A	O	N	B	R	R	D
F	O	P	N	I	D	E	P	O	L	O	R	E	M	L
P	I	Z	A	R	D	I	A	R	I	S	B	I	V	Y
M	L	H	N	I	W	A	S	D	U	C	P	T	W	N
R	A	V	D	R	L	B	M	B	E	I	X	R	T	A
M	T	O	B	A	C	R	M	G	Z	R	S	A	I	M
A	I	P	A	K	O	U	O	A	U	E	T	C	Z	A
G	U	A	C	G	L	R	R	B	W	A	R	B	R	G
E	H	C	U	O	Y	R	C	T	D	A	L	B	D	A
L	U	V	C	L	O	L	M	O	S	R	L	T	U	D
L	O	G	L	A	I	K	P	S	R	C	A	L	B	I
A	R	O	D	W	N	Y	E	J	O	T	N	K	L	D
N	V	I	L	P	I	C	C	U	P	S	E	V	E	S
O	A	H	B	Z	V	P	E	S	N	H	F	S	N	W
S	L	U	E	R	I	C	S	R	E	K	B	H	F	N

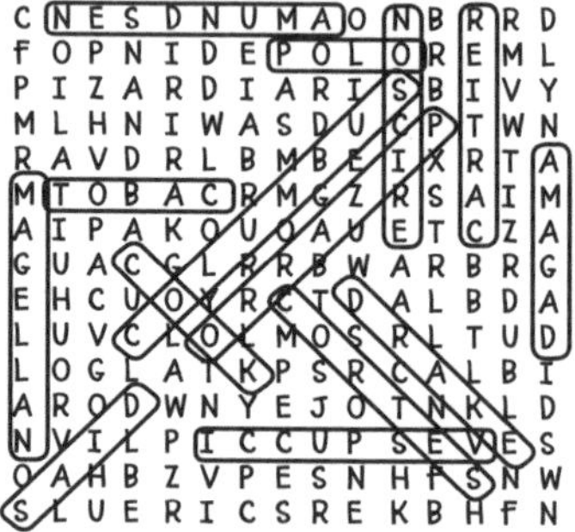

98. Journey quiz:

1. c 2. c 3. a 4. b 5. a 6. b 7. c

100. To the lighthouse:

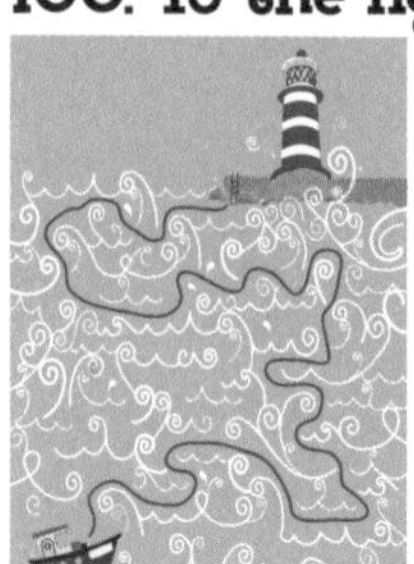

First published in 2016 by Usborne Publishing Ltd, 83-85 Saffron Hill, London EC1N 8RT, England.